To Theo, an inspiration! - J.J.
For Uncle Mark, with all my love - E.W.

First published as *Kisses are Yuk* in 2008
by Hodder Children's Books
This paperback edition published in 2018

Hodder Children's Books
Carmelite House,50 Victoria Embankment
London EC4Y 0DZ

A catalogue record of this book is available
from the British Library.

ISBN: 978 1 444 94717 5

Printed in China

Hodder Children's Books
is a division of Hachette Children's Books
An Hachette UK Company
www.hachette.co.uk

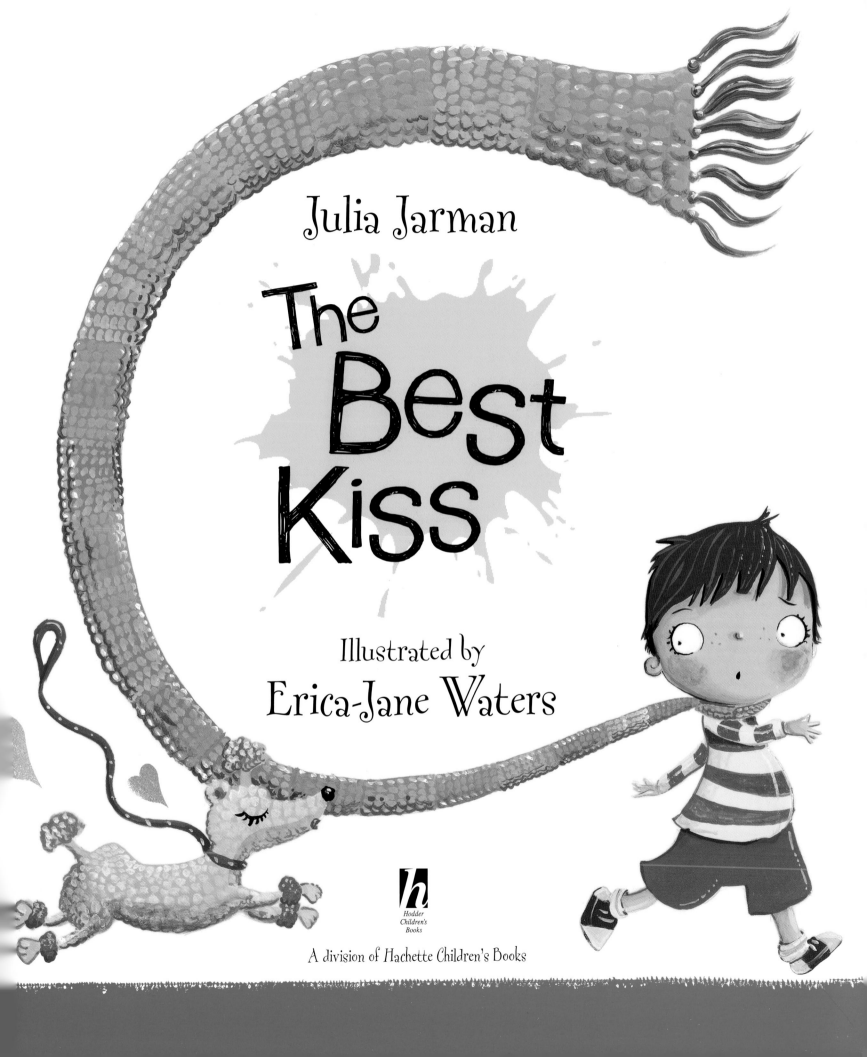

Julia Jarman

The Best Kiss

Illustrated by
Erica-Jane Waters

Hodder
Children's
Books

A division of Hachette Children's Books

There was once a boy called
Jack,

who didn't mind
a pat on the back,

when he scored a **great goal,**

or **jumped** over a pole,

but...

he thought
kisses were
YUK!

He didn't mind a manly
handshake,
when he saved Sue
from the lake,

or when
he saved Klaus
from a burning
house,

but...

he thought kisses were
MUCK!

He quite liked a
'Very well done!
I'm really proud
of you, son,'

when he rescued Brian
from the jaws of a lion.

He loved getting prizes
and
cups
of all
sizes,

but...

DANGER!!
WET ROAD
AHEAD!

kisses were yukky,
kisses were sucky,
kisses were
very,
very
UNLUCKY!

Auntie Poppy's
were sloppy.

Uncle Micky's
were sticky.

Cousin Lily's were horribly licky.

Uncle Henry's were hairy.
Auntie Mary's were scary.

And being kissed
by Great Uncle Russ
was like being kissed
by a very stiff brush.

Uncle Sam
did smackeroos.

Tante Èclaire,
she kissed
in twos.

Granny Groover
kissed
like a hoover.

But worst of all was Auntie Rhonda.

She kissed like an...

So, one night,
Jack made up a rule:
ABSOLUTELY
NO
KISSES
at all...

or stroking my hair,

'I'm
big
and
strong.

I'm
brave
and
tough.

WORLD'S TOUGHEST

Mess
with me
and
I'll get
rough!

Then Jack
climbed into
bed and snuggled
down with...

Growly Ted and Furry Dog and Velvet Rabbit,

for cuddling was his secret habit.

And – **PLEASE** don't tell anyone –
he didn't mind...

a kiss from Mum!

If you enjoyed this humorous story,
you'll love...